SECOND THOUGHTS

By Dr. Lyn Olsen

This book is dedicated to my many great blessings
from God –

The Three Sisters, Aunt Alice, Aunt Donna and my
mom Myrna

My two daughters, Teressa Lyn and Gemavie Marie

My one sister, Rebecca Johnson

And my cousin, Devvi Morgan, who provided
all pictures in the book

CHAPTER 1
CHOICES
(True Story of Love Lost)

Sometimes the most important choices in our lives were the ones we never made. He knew this to be true in his life for once he had a choice but he never made it, and it had haunted him thereafter and defined the rest of his life   Now on this cold December morning as he lay in the hospital bed, having suffered a severe heart attack and not knowing if this was the end or not, there was nothing else he wanted to think about except that which had consumed most of his life.

Laying there in bed, his thoughts went back to where they most often did beginning when he was 17 when life seemed so full of purpose and hope. He had struggled for most of his years since then to forget, but now, as he was grew weaker, he found himself easily succumbing to, even welcoming these thoughts with the hope that if they could not get back his life, then perhaps he could find one last chance.

He could feel that old familiar hollow, disquieting aching inside of him again that he had known since that time which always lingered long after he no longer was thinking about it. He had tried for years to forget and to fill his life with something meaningful, but life had not turned out to be what he had thought it would be. So many times he had sworn to make it right, but neither the time nor place ever seemed quite right, and there never seemed to be the urgency there was now.

Wasting time lying in the hospital bed with the impending eventuality that he might never have another chance filled him with a great dread as though he was like a drug addict unable to give up his addiction that left him wanting it more than ever as the years passed.

With this dread, he felt his grasp loosening on what he had wanted the most. Too ill and tired to fight anymore, he easily succumbed to the thoughts he had wanted as much as he had dreaded them, leaving him wondering why he had ever fought them for they now filled him with the relief he had sought for so long.

It didn't matter to him that nobody came to see him for, although his life did not turn out as expected with loneliness slowly consuming everything, it was the life he had condemned himself to.

The interruptions by the hospital staff had become particularly annoying as it not only seemed they wanted to save him, but it interrupted his dreams which seemed to become more lucid as his illness progressed which seemed to suggest to him he did indeed have one more chance.

CHAPTER 2
A TOWN SOMEWHERE

Andy's and Becky's lives were as harsh and bleak as the small northern town itself where they grew up. Like the townspeople, the town had made them tough and taught them to find hope even in the most hopeless of circumstances with the belief that there would always be another chance.

The town and its people's lives had been toughened by its origins in mining marked by constantly revolving periods fill with periods of scarcity and poverty with some of the harshest and bitterly cold winters that could last almost the entire year with only a reprieve of a month or two of a cool summer.

It was these long bitterly cold winters that made the town seem greyer and bleaker than it might really have been. The cold was heralded by the sinking, ever-darkening thick clouds whose grayness would eventually cloak everything. This grayness was then heightened by the ever-increasing piles of snow that continued to mount throughout the winter, blackened by the sinking dirt from hills left barren by too much mining and the winters that were too cold and too long.

Sitting amongst these hills as large dark monstrous beings
were the huge wooden widow makers that remained forever

vigilant over the town. They had been there from the
beginning of the town, taking the miners deep underground
and sometimes promoting the bleakness of the town when
they did not bring the miners back.

In the beginning, mining had created a booming population
for this town, making it one of the largest in the west. Now
though, the town was a partial remnant of what it used to be
from the too many wars fought over its riches that had won it
the nickname "Richest Hill on Earth." In those wars, many
stole whatever riches they could and left, while others, such
as the companies and unions, continued to fight amongst
themselves forever at the expense of the people and always
leaving nothing behind for them.

While the rest of the world was changing, this town did not
seem to change as the same people continued the same
routines day after day. It sometimes even seemed that the
town was moving backwards in time for the people never
seemed able to get ahead for just as they began to gain, it was

taken away. Sometimes it felt like time stood still, or maybe
was even forgotten, for the days seemed to drag on endlessly
one unto the other.

The only break in the everyday repetitiveness was the
shortening of the days as the grey winter approached, but
more so in the indefatigable hope that the late spring or
summer brought with its revival of the colors from the new
growth on the trees and the wide assortment of wild flowers

reborn from the frozen ground. It was with this same
indefatigable hope that the townspeople approached all of
their troubles despite the reality that things had not changed
much through the years. And it was this same indefatigable
hope that maintained Becky and Andy despite their dark
troubles and deep loneliness.

The bleakness of the town was also reflected in the houses
which were old and weathered, thereby compromising any
attempts at upkeep. Like the town, they, too, had grayed
over the years and decayed at an ever-increasingly faster rate

as evidenced in the crumbling and rotting of their bricks and wood. Most of the houses were two stories with basements oftentimes composed of piled cemented rocks and dirt floors through which the cold dampness seeped even in the summers, but bone-chillingly in the winters.

Perhaps it was intentional that the homes were built close together to share the warmth during the long cold winters and to shelter them from the strong northern winds and the blizzards that oftentimes accompanied them. But perhaps more frequently it was the personal lives of neighbors that was shared.   It was through one particular bedroom window that our story begins.

CHAPTER 3
WINDOWS

When Becky laid across her bed, she could hear most everything that went on next door through her window which looked out onto her neighbor's window. Most of what she heard happened late at night after she had gone to bed, oftentimes waking her up. She wondered if they knew she could hear everything, especially when the father was drunk and very loud. This didn't startle her though because this had been her life before her mom had left dad and moved back to this town where the rest of her family lived, and she knew she couldn't do anything more to help them than she had been able to do for herself.

Although the townspeople always hoped for a better day, today they washed away the ever-constant bleakness of the town and their troubles by drinking, and this was what had stolen her life and now stole through her window. Even for those who tried to get away from this, as her family had, the alternative was oftentimes as lonely and destitute.

But despite the lack of being unable to help, it still frightened her to hear the drunken rages of the parents next door as it served to remind her of what she had lived through every night for many years as a small and unknowing child. She remembered how frightened she became when she would hear her father's footsteps coming up the stairs, but bravely overcoming her worst fears she would rush to stand between her mother and siblings and their drunk father in order to stop any beatings.

Despite the harshness of their life now, she could still feel her heart break when she recollected the last time she had seen her father. The whole family had moved away for a few years from this town with the hopes that things would get better with her father's job promotion, but his drinking worsened and soon thereafter they returned without him. She remembered as though it was yesterday his trembling shoulders and tears streaking his cheeks. She never had a doubt that he had loved them all, more than anything else, but it had not been enough to give him the strength to make the choice he desperately wanted to make but never could.

CHAPTER 4
FENCES

Fairy tales are oftentimes a depiction of real life, and so it
was in Becky's. With her dad gone and her mom working
several minimum wage jobs which was not enough to feed all
of them some days, it left too much for her mother to do.
Without having to be asked, the obligation fell upon Becky to
keep the house and feed her siblings. This was an obligation
that Becky had willingly taken on out of her love for her
mother with the hope that she could make her mom happy
and stop her tears that she oftentimes cried when she thought
nobody could hear. But it was a sacrifice that went unnoticed
and unappreciated; instead it was oftentimes met with
demeaning words and actions that demolished her self-worth
from her siblings, and after these derogations had been said
enough times, Becky was convinced that they had always
been true, leaving her to wonder what awful things she must
had done as a child to cause this.

Her everyday routine consisted of cleaning and cooking until late at night, and then getting up early to walk miles to school in even the worst of weather, leaving her with little time to meet her own needs. Where she did find solace was in school though because she excelled there and nobody bothered her, although that was in large part due to the fact that nobody noticed her. It was this isolation she suffered at home and at school that left her feeling she would never be good enough for someone to like, but least of all to love.

Becky could be described as plain then, but this was due in large part to her having greater concerns than her looks. She had long brown hair that could look good on other girls but hers instead hung thin and parted on its own accord straight down the middle, but it didn't matter because she always pulled it back into a ponytail. Her eyes were hazel like most other people, so overall she appeared very average at a cursory glance.

She had always struggled with weight her whole life, never seeming to be skinny enough, she was sure, to ever be considered pretty like other girls. As plain as she seemed to be, her clothes were even plainer for it was only on her birthdays that she received a new outfit. So most often she wore the same things, a simple white shirt with blue brushed cotton pants. Without much time or money to invest in clothes or looks and believing that nobody noticed her anyways, she didn't worry much about her appearance as it seemed like a waste of time.

Strengthened by the challenges of her difficult life, what she didn't invest in her looks and popularity she devoted to being kind to others, even to the fault of sacrificing herself which perhaps was viewed by some as a weakness but which, in truth, left her prone to misperceptions by others. It didn't matter to her though what others thought because she knew what was most important in her life was who she was, and if she stopped caring, then she felt she would have lost her soul.

Out of her generosity, she hoped that someday someone would be able to love her. But the more she talked about these feelings, she more she was ridiculed and the worse it got. From this, she learned that the only defense that seemed to work was silence, so she never complained and she never asked for anything. And the silence seemed to work because the cruelness seemed to diminish, or perhaps she had grown

numb to it. And the silence seemed to work because she didn't have to endure disappointment when her dreams didn't come true and she again faced rejection. In truth, this was a poor choice that would haunt her throughout her life and too often spoil the choices she made, or should have made.

While her life may have seemed harsh, oftentimes these kinds of times can make a person better, and so it was for Becky though she could not imagine it then. Her harsh times was fostering great compassion and forgiveness in her so that everyone who knew here would always be better.

Despite her compassion for others, her lonely life had kept her isolated which complicated her ability to understand how to relate to others. Unable to alleviate her loneliness, she filled up her time with, not only school and taking care of the house, but also with music, books, and long walks undeterred by even the coldest and cruelest of weather for it brought great relief and reflection. Through these, she could remove herself from her present circumstances and immerse herself in faraway places where dreams came true and where she could imagine that someone would love her one day.

Her world was made livable but filling her head with these words of songs and books to push out the world where nobody loved her, and to keep alive her hope that one day someone would.   But music in particular spoke to her of promises of love for even the loneliest of people, like herself.

> Angel of my life time,
> Answer to all answers I can find….
> I would love you, build my world around you
> Never leave you 'til my life is done
> Baby, I love you…
> Come into my arms
> Let me know the wonder of all of you
> (Barry Manilow)

CHAPTER 5
SEPARATE LIVES

Becky's window that looked out into her neighbor's house looked into Andy's world. His world had not changed like hers, but yet it was still the same world they shared. Although they said nothing to each other and, therefore, never acknowledging what they knew about each other, it was these deepest secrets that wafted across the space between the windows that forged a greater intimacy between them than most people ever shared with another. It was ethereal, like the people we pass in life while never knowing the importance they would one day possess in our life.

The worlds they shared were full of the same troubles for their fathers were more drunk than not. But while her world didn't contain that trouble anymore, Andy's was still enveloped in this darkness which Becky oftentimes could hear through their windows. What they also shared was the same hope that one day life would be better, but neither at this time imagined that their hope for a better day might lie within each other.

While their worlds were similar in some ways, they were also separate in other ways. Whereas nobody seem to even notice Becky at school, Andy was arguably the most popular boy in school and he was always involved in everything which suited him well as it kept him most often away from home. For him, what was past for Becky, he was still living with the fighting and drunkenness of his father, and sometimes his mother as well. Whereas she had found her solace in books, music and walks which did not require being gone from home, for him the solution was to be gone as much as he could. So, he threw himself into everything that kept him away from home including being prom king and football quarterback which mystified Becky as she could not fathom being popular.

Being popular for Andy meant most of the girls liked him and were always hanging around him which made Becky wonder which one was his girlfriend for that day as there always seemed to be so many of them. It also made Becky wonder if she would ever be able to be like that and flirt like they did for she was acutely aware of her awkwardness when around others, especially boys.

Like Becky, Andy was not exceptionally good-looking but his personality seemed to override any physical faults he may have had. His hair was brown and his eyes were brown. He wasn't the tallest boy at five feet ten inches, but being in sports, he spent a great deal of time working out, and it showed in his lean muscular body. But what Becky thought seemed to be most charming about him was his extraordinary sense of the needs of others and his quickness to help them.

Therefore, it was no surprise to her that of anybody, Andy was the one person who seemed to notice her on occasion, although rather informally and briefly. To her, kindness was the most attractive virtue anyone could have and, in her mind, he showed it more than anyone. She remembered one time in particular at school when nobody else would help an old man who was trying to push a big old car up a hilly road with his old wife trying to steer it. Though many people watched, without hesitating Andy pulled a couple of his friends with him and helped.

In their two very separate worlds, neither of them imagined that their worlds would ever collide.   Mixed with her intimate knowledge of his life at home and her admiration of his kindness, it was understandable why she found herself thinking of him often in ways she imagined other girls thought about him, but which she herself had never thought of before.

Although he seemed to her to have the best of worlds and would never have thought twice about her, in truth he was discontented with the way of his life. The life he had created was his way of hiding away from his problems, but this did not diminish his desire to find hope and meaning in his life that had been straggled with too many broken promises and dreams already.

CHAPTER 6
NEIGHBORS

Without knowing, Andy nurtured the little hope Becky had that someone might someday like her by his nodding his head when he saw her at home or school. She hesitantly would smile back uncertain and afraid that he might not have meant it for her or that he thought what a fool she was.

Sometimes she would let herself daydream that there was a purpose behind the nod of his head, and that he thought about her maybe once in a while. At times these daydreams seemed very real as she thought she caught him watching her intently as though there really was something, if not attractive, then perhaps interesting about her, though she couldn't imagine what it might be. Although she always quickly dismissed this as part of her daydreaming and longing, it still left her with a sense of warmth along with a feeling of awkwardness for she could not comprehend the meaning.

It was late one night that it all seemed terribly bad at his True to his good ways, Becky could hear Andy shuffling his siblings out of the room and then remaining to hopefully thwart any more trouble. Without realizing it, it was moments like this that seemed to strengthen her feelings for him. But likewise, these moments were gut-wrenching because they brought back too many similar memories in her own recent past, and it kept her awake, thinking, all night.

Having thus spent an emotional and restless night, Becky woke early having thought most of the night of what she could do to let him know how much she admired his courage, but what she refused to acknowledge was how much she cared about him. She feared letting him know she really cared because she not only had never felt that way about a boy before, but she was certain he would reject her if he knew what she really thought about him.

So she turned to the one thing she knew that always seemed to make things better and which she did well, she baked a chocolate cake. But once the cake was done and frosted, she wasn't sure what to do next because she had not contemplated the dread in having to take the cake over to his house and what he might suspect. But her desire to let him know much he meant to her, and her compassion for him

having to endure what she once had, overrode her fear and drove her to the front porch of his house. As she walked towards his house she began to hope that he wouldn't answer the door, but this was conflicted by a gnawing feeling of disappointment if he did not answer the door.

Standing before his door, she knocked quietly at his door as though it could subdue any awkwardness or embarrassment she felt. She waited few moments, trying to decide if she should run or not while rehearsing the whole time the few words she might say.

Within a few moments, she heard someone coming, and thought, "That chance is lost, I can't turn and run now" although she could feel her feet still wanting to run away as if they had become filled with the leaden dread that filled her gut as well.

She stood her ground bravely as the door opened, but felt her heart go faint as Andy looked out at her. She no longer remembered anything that she had practiced to say and felt woefully inadequate standing there with her stupid chocolate cake. "He does think I am a fool," she thought as she watched the expression on his face.

Though many thoughts had flown through her mind in the short time she had stood there, he didn't hesitate and opened the door wide. With his cute smirk that she had noticed many times before when he would nod at her, and which she had come to adore, he asked, "Heh Becky, what you got?"

Still, he stood there, staring at her in the way she had imagined and hoped that one day he might for there seemed to be no ridicule or disgust evident on his face, but in the next moment she wondered if he stared without saying anything because he enjoyed putting her through misery.

"All for me?" he teased her. It felt like torture to her which she had always kinda expected because she was never going to be good enough for someone like him to think about.

"Of course," she mumbled, while never looking up. Realizing what she had really said, her discomfort grew intolerable and she began to contemplate turning and running, no matter how embarrassing it might be, and now she wished she had really run earlier.

She stammered, "Well, I meant.. for all you." But again she faltered miserably, "I mean, I thought it would make you happy." Now she wondered if it was actually possible for her to melt in between the wooden slats of the porch for those words seemed even dumber than what she had said before.

Forever after this, she wondered what his response really was, but she thought he said, "I wouldn't want to share you." "He must have meant the cake," she thought.

As he took the cake from her, he smiled at her with his smile that she always believed could melt anyone's heart and solve any problems she ever had, but for this one moment she let herself believe and enjoy that this time his smile was meant just for her. She wondered if he knew what his smile meant in her lonely world where for there had been far too little.

CHAPTER 7
SOMETHING MORE

After this first personal encounter between them, things didn't seem quite as awkward between them. Andy more often passed her locker at school, saying some kind of hello. She mused, "He is nice to everyone," because she could not imagine he thought anything else of her, so just as quickly as she began to let herself ponder the thrill of thinking he might like her, she dashed it with the thought "he would never like anyone like me." But sometimes she let these thoughts and her accompanying feelings fill her daydreams for it seemed that every day his presence and few small words gave her greater comfort and warmth.

So it was highly unbeknownst to her that Andy's jaunts past her school locker were purposeful for he had imagined and wondered for a long time about her. But while it seemed so easy to him to be with other girls, he found her very perplexing for she never acted nor responded the way the other girls did when he flirted with them, seemingly turning away when he approached. This left him feeling unsure of himself and filled him with an awkwardness he had never felt before with a girl. And so just as quickly he would turn his course away from her as though he had intended to go somewhere else but this left him more frustrated because he wasn't able to do that he really wanted to do.

When he pondered his frustrating predicament, he rationalized, "She would never like anyone like me because she is too good and sweet." Unknowingly, with these perceptions he had failed to realize that she was not experienced in dating, and so her awkwardness could easily rival his.

When he pondered his frustrating predicament, he rationalized, "She would never like anyone like me because she is too good and sweet." Unknowingly, with these perceptions he had failed to realize that she was not experienced in dating, and so her awkwardness could have easily rival his.

To alleviate his frustration, he began to try to create more opportunities to be with her but their worlds were quite different as she was not one of the popular kids and so in her world girls like her didn't have the luxury of choosing who they could talk to or be with, so no real opportunities presented themselves at all. Despite the lack of any opportunities to spend time together, though, it didn't stop their imaginings and for her she now found that time spent with her music and books had become clouded with thoughts of him. For him, his awkwardness around her seemed to grow more, so he found himself constantly evaluating and judging the few words he said to her and regretting so many of them after he had said them or didn't say them.

CHAPTER 8
IN THE EVENING

In the early summer of her 17th birthday when the nights finally began to warm slightly, Becky could be found more often sitting on her front porch, watching the people go by with whom she never had much contact but oftentimes imagined their whole life stories.

She found this so entrancing that she contemplated focusing her future college studies on psychology for the past and present lives and struggles of people fascinated her. When she would go to a museum or old town, she would imagine all of the troubles and joys that must have happened in the lives long gone as she walked around, touching everything as others so many years before must have. She would also think about what kind of position she would have had and how she could have helped others, even long ago.

Andy seemed less in a hurry this summer to be gone all of the time, and so the two of them could be found sitting together late into the evening on one of their porches talking about everything, from the least important to the deepest questions that wore at a person's soul.

It was a far greater joy for Andy that he ever thought there ever could be. "Talking with her," Andy thought, "seems so easy now and much easier than with any other girl. I never feel like I have to weigh my words or think twice before I say something. Even if I say something that doesn't come out right, she never seems to mind, but rather seems to understand what I meant and I don't have to always be explaining myself. She always seems to accept it as having been said with the best of intentions."

Having someone to talk to didn't change how Becky felt about herself nor what she imagined others thought of her, so despite their long talks, she never imagined that Andy ever thought of her as anything other than the girl next door for he didn't act the same around her as he did with the other girls. This behavior of his led her to surmise that she lacked what other girls had which, she thought, is why boys, and in particular Andy, were never interested in her. But she had an even greater fear as she grew more comfortable with their evening chats which was that one day he would realize what everyone else knew and would stop spending time with her.

Quite the contrast and with complete obliviousness by Becky, Andy oftentimes mused, "How can she not know that I could be elsewhere or with someone else but I choose to be with her. She acts as though she doesn't know how I feel thought I have made it very plain. Why is that what charmed other girls seems to elicit no response from her?"

As their evenings spent together continued on, Andy grew to understand Becky more with the realization that she wasn't like other girls, but rather how special she was. He also realized that she made him happy when nobody else could. "No matter what happens in my life," he would contemplate, "I know that I could never be happier than I am now with her."

But with a lifetime of uncertainty fostered in both of them, both of them remained oblivious to how they felt about each other, and said nothing; perhaps because they never acknowledged their feelings, or perhaps even more probable that they themselves did not comprehend their own feelings for each other so all remained unsaid.

As their nights continued on much the same, their talk became easier and easier as their trust in each other grew. Even the silences were no longer disturbing or difficult for oftentimes they shared the same thoughts without having to speak them. But as young people are wont to do, the sameness every night had led to their nonchalance which harbored a forgetfulness that things could change some day.

CHAPTER 9
SPOKEN WORDS

As the summer days lengthened, so did their time together although for them time seemed to no longer have any meaning as it seemed to stand still as though nothing would ever change.

On one particular evening an opportunity arose for them to tell each other how they felt. While they often talked about the things they could never talk to anyone else about, their conversations had never become intimate with the sharing of their true feelings for each other.

As though a quiet prelude to what might follow, their conversation was quite mundane as though both were preoccupied with avoiding what they really wanted to say. For Andy, he had been trying to find the courage to tell Becky what he had never told any girl before of his feelings for her, but he had been afraid to tell her because he wasn't sure how she would react. Over these summer months his respect and feelings for her had deepened greatly and he didn't want to destroy what they had between them by saying the wrong thing and ending it forever, for she was not like other girls.

As the night wore on and their hesitation kept them from speaking of what they wanted most to say, fear began to grip them that perhaps time could slip by too quickly and they would find many years later that they never said what they wanted most. This fear and the stilted mundane nature of their talk left too much silence between them, heightening their confusion and creating doubt as to how the other would respond with even the possibility of rejection. As close as their friendship had grown, this frightened them both because they didn't want to lose what had become the best part of their life, for it would have been better to have something with each other than nothing at all.

He had wanted desperately for such a long time to tell her what he had never felt about any other girl, that he had fallen hopelessly in love with her. "Why," he wondered, "did it always seem so easy to talk to her about everything else, but more difficult than ever before with any other girl to tell her how I feel about her?"

As the night grew late and the finality of the evening loomed near, he could feel the old fear that time could be lost forever creeping upon him, so he grew bolder. Struggling as he had done many times before, he tried once again to lead their conversation towards their feelings by asking her what was most important to her or what she liked most about guys, but her response was nothing that he would ever have imagined.

"I want to matter to someone, enough that someone could love me enough to think I was beautiful, "she quietly murmured. "But no guy would ever like me."

He could feel his thoughts and feelings began to tumble crazily in his head as he struggled for his response. Thoughts kept piling on top of each other so quickly that he found himself unable to response for he had never imagined anyone ever saying these words.

Despite his confusion and hesitancy, what he felt the most was his heart breaking because he realized the pain in her heart that he most certainly must have been a part of it, at the least in not doing anything to alleviate it. He thought to himself, "She should never have been left to feel this way ever in her life," and he feel the guilt blanketing him for having never said anything to her despite always wanting to. What he finally understood was that what he had perceived as her disinterest in him was because she didn't think he

would ever like her, but even more so that nobody ever
would.

Feeling that he had let her down, he found it even harder now
to say what he had always wanted to say. Although he felt he
knew her better than anyone he had ever known, more than
ever now he wanted to give the rest of his life to her so that
he could ensure she would never feel alone or unloved again.

But even more importantly at that moment he realized that he
didn't want the life that other guys seemed to want where
there always lots of girls. He reflected, "Why would I want
any other woman after having known the best, and knowing
that she always made me happier than I ever imagined."
While recognizing his strong feelings for her, his own shades
of unworthiness crept in to remind him that perhaps he was
not good enough for her.

While his thoughts raced and he remained in silence, she
began doubting and chastised herself for having said
something she should never have said. She wondered how
she could recoup what might prove to be her greatest loss.

"It's the same as always," she thought. "I should have been
silent, I should never have said anything. Every time I open
myself up, it always ends disastrously. What I said was
much too close to my heart and its pain, and no one wants to
know that. He now sees what everyone has always seen in
me, and why nobody wants to be with me. I can see it in his
face and his silence," she lamented. "I have lost my only
friend, perhaps my true love."

As the seconds lapsed, dazed and confused and still uncertain
what to say, he reacted rather than thinking. Placing his
hands on each cheek of hers and drawing his face close to
hers, he most quietly said, "Becky, I have always thought
you were the most beautiful girl I have ever known."

CHAPTER 10
IMMEMORABLE

The warm light summer breeze of the evenings tickled over her skin and through her hair as they sat on their porches which heightened the same sense of the warm comfort between them.   It was on one of those evenings in early July, while making small talk that Andy told Becky, "My birthday is coming soon." Teasingly, he asked, "What are you getting me?'

Becky hadn't thought about such a thing, for she had never had money to buy a birthday gift for someone else, least of all for a boy. With clueless discomfort, she replied, "How could I get you something?"

Sensing her growing discomfort, he quickly changed the subject but unfortunately asked a more sensitive question that made her even more uncomfortable, "When is your birthday?"

He watched her and waited, but she avoided his eyes instead. He thought to himself and wondered how, once again, her response was never what he thought it would be, especially to such a simple question. He could feel his frustration mounting for it seemed sometimes that the most unexpected words or actions were potentially confounding his hopes. He was even more baffled because he had thought birthdays were important, especially for girls, and he thought remembering hers would show her how much he cared.

With no response from her, Andy persisted with irritation, "Well, are you going to tell me at least that?"

Feeling pressured, she quietly groaned. In his persistence to know, he remained incognizant that for her it was something far greater that she didn't want to acknowledge, let alone talk about.

Out of his growing frustration and sensing her unwavering discomfort, he laughed as a way to distract her. When she didn't respond, he spoke again with regret slipping off his tongue as he said the words, "It seems that while I tell you everything about myself, you say too little about yourself, and I want to know you. I'm tired of trying because I don't know what I should have said when you respond with nothing."

Unsure what to say to express her feelings, she thought, "Some things people shouldn't ask about because they are hard to talk about." He continued to grow more exasperated for never had a girl been less responsive to his attempts to care. However, if he had looked deeper into her eyes, he would have seen the tears filling them up, and then he would have been able to share the lifetime of sorrow that lay deep in her soul.

This simple question indeed embodied a great deal of sorrow for Becky throughout her life. For too many years, her birthdays had not mattered to anyone and no one had celebrated them. Presents had been few over the years and cakes oftentimes missing. His questions had allowed what had laid hidden in her to resurface along with her fear that he would one day realize that he had wasted his time with her, so she resorted to the one place of comfort she had learned, to be silent.

While it may not have been fair that he should suffer because of her past, at this moment, nonetheless she did not have control over her feelings that arose at the renewal of painful memories that had reminded her all of her life that no matter what she did or who she was, she would never be good enough for anyone. These feelings always left her feeling as though she was paying for something she did wrong when very young but which she never knew.

Her sorrow was also complicated by the fact that her birthday had already slipped by without anyone acknowledging it for it had been two days before. She had let herself hope before her birthday that this birthday might have been different but it wasn't. She consoled herself, thinking why should it have been any different for this summer seemed more like a figment of her imagination and that once school began, he would be back with his friends.

There they sat for a few more, very awkward moments in silence, but still they didn't leave because despite the seemingly harsh words and silence between them, at this moment neither wanted to leave the other. It was not until the dusk was replaced with the still darkness of the night that Andy slipped away, and she wondered if she would see him ever again.

CHAPTER 11
JUST ANOTHER DAY

It had been a restless night for Becky. She imagined that Andy probably had slept well, oblivious to the turmoil and pain he had awoken in her. She had reminder herself all night, "I knew sooner or later he would not come back. Just another day like all the others in my life now."

She had thought she had grown accustomed and quite well adjusted to being alone, but her thoughts belied her feelings because this time she felt much more alone and it seemed to hurt much more than it ever had before. It felt as though a scar had healed over her wound of loneliness during the summer nights with him, but now it had been ripped off.

She had no doubt that he would avoid her, for surely now he understood what everyone else had known about her and why she would never be good enough for him. So, while she was usually up early cleaning on Sundays, this morning she didn't want to get out of bed. Instead, she lay there staring out into his window, but there was nothing to see or hear coming from the window. This absence dashed her struggling hope that she could undo what she did not understand from last night, and that he would let her know everything was going to be okay.

Finally, knowing that she couldn't let her mother down by leaving the house a mess with dishes most probably piling even higher as she lay there, she poured herself out of bed as though it was done without any conscious effort by her for she felt drained of everything. She was very tired today, not just physically tired, but emotionally tired of missing out on everything and never knowing how to change that. She was tired of being the one who was always suppose to care when nobody else did, of always having to do what nobody else wanted to do, and especially tired of nobody caring about her.

As she continued to reflect, she realized that now, once again, she would be alone with nothing to do anymore, nowhere to go, no one to talk to. She had not realized how their summer evenings had filled up her days with the happiness she had hoped for so long, but which she apparently was just as guilty of not appreciating or holding on to until it was gone.

The house seemed quiet as she slipped downstairs at this late morning hour, for it was almost 10, a time which she hardly ever slept past and a time when the rest of her siblings would still be in bed.

Intently, she remained quiet with the hope that it would wake nobody so there could be time when the house was quiet and even stayed clean after she was done. Immersed in her efforts to be quiet and in her thoughts about how things had worsened so quickly, she rounded the corner of the stairs and turned to go into the kitchen which was past the living room.

She was so intently immersed in her thoughts that she collided with Andy surrounded by some of his and her family and friends, and in his hands was the most beautifully decorated birthday cake she imagined she had ever seen.

Quickly and quite naturally her face reddened, partly because of her overwhelming surprise, but also because she was fighting the tears that welled up in her eyes. Standing before her as no one had ever done before for her was the one person she had doubted so severely all night and morning. With the harshness and loneliness she had endured for most of her, she thought she had learned to not cry, but now it felt as though all of her hidden and long-lost feelings rushed out of her at once, and she began to cry.

Although she had certainly dreamed of such a day and even practiced what she might say and do, nothing in those dreams seemed to fit this situation. So, she stood there, but this time she let herself enjoy the rush of her feelings and the tears which she no longer fought to silence, and she wondered how she had ever done without them for so long.

Just as quickly though, she became fearful because she didn't want the present to end as the previous night had when she had said nothing. But she hesitated for she wasn't sure still what she should say, especially to him in front of everyone else because what she was really feeling was much stronger than anything she had ever felt before. And she didn't know how to find the courage to share her intense feelings and joy with others, especially him.

But Andy didn't hesitate. He walked towards her with the cake as everyone sang "Happy Birthday," and when he was close to her, he smiled, bent over and lingeringly kissed her on the cheek.

If Becky had more experience with relationships, perhaps she would have then and there realized that what had been building for months inside of her and what she felt at that moment for Andy was an intimacy that few men ever know with the woman they love. And if Andy could have seen into her heart at that moment, he would never have let her leave him ever again.

CHAPTER 12
ONE SUMMER NIGHT

Their summer nights continued to slide by without urgency without them speaking much more about their emotional evening, but having each other there seemed to be all that

they felt they would ever need. But what they particularly did not speak of yet was how what they felt inside was changing.

With the lengthening sunshine that accompanied the longer summer days the warmth lasted further into the evenings. With little money in their pockets and the whole night to spend together, they decided one late afternoon to make a change and take a long walk. Becky grinned, wondering if Andy knew what a long walk meant for her as she had spent long hours walking as they had always been one of her favorite ways to find peace.

The grin on her face put a smile on his face too, for it gave him great satisfaction that she found comfort with him being there just as he found comfort in her being there. As though driven with some dread that if they waited too long, the evening would slip away, they didn't hesitate to leave.

What was most amiable about their long walk was that, even when they didn't talk, it was just as pleasant as when they did, and perhaps more importantly reaffirming because they were together. As Andy walked along, he mused, "With other girls, silence had always been painful because I felt like I had to entertain them, weighing every word and everything I did, but not with her. With her, every moment is precious and an eternity of them may not be enough."

On they walked together, half in musing within their own thoughts and half in idle chatter such as talk about the brilliant sunset which was one thing this town could be proud of. The town's sunsets were usually filled with the widest spectrum of brilliant colors as it slipped down over the mountain tops. Sometimes the last final grasp of the sunset would be captured in the streaks of colored light that would reach through the clouds so brilliantly that they darkened everything that lay beneath it.

While their talk was not serious tonight, it still retained the warmth of the great friendship that had developed between them. After walking awhile, thinking the whole time of how to make it last longer, Andy suggested, "Would it be too far to walk all the way to the flats and get a pizza?" We can sit there and relax until they close, then walk back." She didn't say anything for she loved walking, especially now that she didn't have to walk alone. Rather she smiled with warm acquiescence which left him beguiled as to how seemingly easy it was for her to make him happy without having done or said a thing.

But Becky had not have anticipated what would happen when they got there, and she wondered if Andy had even considered it too. As he opened the door to the place, it was quickly evident that most of his friends, the popular kids, were there.

"While Andy may have said hello to me in school, showing up with me tonight at this place in front of everyone is definitely a terrible mistake," as she wondered what the outcome would be.   Contemplating all of this made Becky freeze from the uncertainty and wonder if she could disappear so that this would never happen, and if not that, slide away as though they were together, thereby saving him his pride.

Before she could think any more, he grabbed her hand and pulled her next to him.

While she had never really cared what others thought of her because she knew she couldn't change that, she did worry about what others would think of him for she never wanted to make things worse for him, and he did have his reputation to protect.

"After all of our time together this summer," she thought, "this is an awful way for it to all end, especially because it was so unexpected, thus leaving us no time to cherish what was to become our last few moments."   She felt as if sudden death had overwhelmed their summer and grieved her that she had not prepared better for this moment. What made her saddest, though, was the realization that what they had enjoyed that summer had to end sometime, something she had refused to acknowledge at all., but here it was that moment now when her summer would end.

While no one at school had ever seemed to notice her, she felt as though every eye in the place was watching her now. Andy waved at his friends and continued towards a table away from them where they would be alone. Not sure how she felt, his thoughts were about her for he didn't want to make her feel uncomfortable by having to make small talk with others she didn't know and he didn't know if she even liked them. But mostly he didn't want to share his time with her because it was most precious to him and he felt as though he might never have enough time with her.

As she sat on one side of the table, he sat on the other, watching her without saying anything. While she thought about how selfish she had been during the summer in not thinking about what was important to him, he too seemed to be deep in thought. "Funny," she mused, "we are probably both thinking the same thing of how uncomfortable this is for him and how embarrassing I am."

Shortly after sitting down, he got up and left, crossing the room to where his friends were. As he did so, she began to strategize how she could sneak out. He quickly became engaged in talking with his friends.

Several girls then joined the group and one in particular, snuggled up close to him, putting her arm through his. Becky had seen this girl many times at school with him, and now she sat frozen, wishing she could somehow vanish into thin air, but on the other hand, wishing she could be a small mouse listening to everything they said, and in particular what the girl was saying to him.

Watching this, Becky wondered who the girl really was for Andy never talked about any other girls. She wondered, "Why can't I be like her? Why do I find it so hard to know what to do?" The tension within Becky continued to mount as she watched and wondered what they must be saying about her, but perhaps they had already forgotten her.

While her thoughts had gone in one direction, Andy's had gone in quite another direction. Surrounded by his friends, he was thinking only of Becky. As he stared at the other girls, it became even more apparent to him how special Becky was, and he once again reaffirmed that he never wanted to lose her.

For Becky, it seemed like hours had gone by since he left her. Although she had spent many a night walking alone in complete solitude, she became wistful at the thought of how lonely this walk home tonight would be without him. As she bolstered herself despite the tears that began to fill her eyes for her journey alone, she realized the urgency of doing something sooner rather than later to ensure the least embarrassment.

In truth, it had been less than fifteen minutes before Andy returned with two sodas. This time he slid in next to her. As he pulled himself closer to her, she wondered if he could feel her heart beating louder and faster at that moment with her pulse racing as if in fear for what she had planned to do but which was now thwarted or for the feeling that overwhelmed her at that moment with him so near.

With a rush of warmth that filled her heart, she wished for the smoothness of words and actions that other girls seemed so easily to do. Instead, she was filled with anguish in trying to decide how she could do what the other girls most assuredly would have done at that moment, snuggling up close him and touching him gently so he would know how much he meant to her at that moment.

So they sat there together, talking in the ways they always did, and only when the place was closing, did they get up to leave. Hopeful that his friends were gone, she was greatly dismayed to see a few of his friends had remained and joined them as they walked out the door

His friends walked quite a ways with them, treating her as nonchalantly as if she had always been a part of their group. "How strange," she thought. "For all of the time I have thought I was alone, it feels now like I was never alone nor that I never did not know how to be so." Inside of her, a joy stirred that maybe someday things would be better.

Since they had walked a long ways, they eventually were once again alone. As the evening breeze picked up a slight chill, he moved closer to her, putting his arm around her to keep her warm. How quiet the night seemed, and so they walked silently as though fearing to break the silence because it would surely break this   tender moment they shared together.

CHAPTER 13
SEPARATE WAYS

With time seeming to have stood still during the summer and believing that these moments might last forever, Becky and Andy spent their summer in an oblivious state of informality about their future, and so they had made no plans. Though they had hoped it would last forever, a summer is a very short time period, and so now that fall had returned it was gone.   Perhaps afraid to disturb the summer's solace they had known, they had ignored and did not heed the inevitable change that was to come their senior year nor considered the possibility that it could even foretell that one day they might not be there for each other.

Their time together still remained important to them, but being important and having the time for it apparently were not the same thing as it became much harder for them to find the time.   The bitter cold that was starting to seep into the nights also compromised their chances to be together as there had never been anywhere else for them to meet other than on their front porches. With the informality of their times together, their resolve to meet began to wear away aggravated by their feeling that they had little control over it

In September, Andy started a job after school at a local drugstore where the owner, who was also the pharmacist, had known his family a long time.   With his new-found money, one of the first things he bought was a used Camaro which served to heighten his popularity even more, particularly with girls who were seen oftentimes visiting the pharmacy perhaps too often. Seeing these girls flirting with him brought reality back for Becky of who she was not and who he was. But it also mystified her greatly because she still understood little about how these girls attracted the boys, and she wondered if she would ever know and if any guy would ever like her the way they liked the other girls.

Several months after that, Becky found a job at a fabric store. With her money from her job, she was also finally able to start buying clothes and other such things which greatly showed in her ever-improving appearance, which did not go unnoticed by others in her school. Although she did not recognize it, the change that was most important for Becky, though, was what happened inside of her when Andy first told her she was beautiful.

Most important, with her money, although she certainly could not afford a car, Becky bought a bike. Never complaining, she had spent years walking several miles back and forth every day to school and now walking to work which was another several miles. So, for her, the bike was long-awaited and long-needed and perhaps just as appreciated as his car.

Only a month had passed since she had brought her bike which had saved her much time and grief as her trips were much shorter and thus less cold. She had gone outside to get her bike and head off to work one Saturday morning, only to find that her bike was not there. Perplexed, she didn't think at first that anyone would have taken it because nobody worried about locking their doors or anything else in this small town for everyone knew everyone else.

Thus, her first thoughts were that she must have put it elsewhere and forgotten, but her search was to no avail, and she began to suspect that it had been stolen. She was standing there dumbfounded when Andy yelled from his porch, "Becky, aren't you going to be late?"

"I don't know where it is, I can't find my bike," she asked as if a question to him for which she hoped he had a good answer.

She replied to her own question, "I don't think I did anything with it. I remember coming home late last night from work and putting it on the porch as I always did, but it's not here, and I'm going to be late for work. I don't know what to do or where to look that I haven't already."

Andy and Becky's schedules at school and work had always been different which had contributed to their lack of opportunities to spend time with each other and it was also why he had never offered her rides although he had wanted very much to do so. She also seemed so determined to get her bike and, as she seemed wont to do, she was rather independent, preferring to do things on her own which oftentimes undermined Andy's efforts to do things for her.

"Now seems like the right time to ask," he thought. So, just as quickly so she couldn't make a decision otherwise, he asked, "Can I give you a ride?"

"In your car?" she asked. She had thought part of the reason they had not spent much time together since school began was because his popularity had only increased with his having a car and so he was spending more time with his friends and all of the girls who always surrounded him. Despite these thoughts, she still imagined how great it would have been to ride in his car.

Despite her misgivings about his intentions, sometimes desperation is the creator of some of the greatest opportunities, so bewildered and desperate to get to work, she acquiesced without any argument.

With his keys in hand, he jumped proudly and quickly into his car for he feared that he if he hesitated he might lose this opportunity as he seemed to do too often with her. Swinging the door open for her, she slid in and smiled with her smile that always made him feel like when he was with her he was the best he would ever be.

Without having to ask, when work ended that night, he was there waiting for her. They didn't go straight home that night though for nobody was waiting for them at home anyways. Instead he took her for a drive outside of the town.

Only a few minutes in this rural town took a person out into the wild country where towering mountains with lakes nestled underneath were plentiful. With winter approaching, the bright full moon played off of the low-hanging clouds that foreshadowed the nearness of the bitter coldness in its mixing of shadows of dark and white within them, and their tumultuous building of layers of puffiness as the wind tossed them about.

"Are you cold, Becky?" he asked as he began to roll up the windows?"

"No, please," she responded excitedly. "Leave the windows down. I love it when the wind rushes through my hair, swirling it around my face and tickling my neck."

In the weeks that followed, although they looked for it, her bike was never found. It was certain that a neighbor had stolen it, and Becky thought, "Who could have needed that bike more than me? Why did they steal from the one person who had the least and needed it the most?"   She sighed, thinking, "I'll have to return to walking the long miles to and from school and work no matter what kind of weather."

The next night, Sunday, before the school week began, Andy came over and told her, "I'm always there for you, Becky. I'll take you wherever you need to go. If I go in early or if you stay late, we can wait for each other."

"You don't mind?" she asked him.

"I never minded waiting for you," and he wondered if he should add that he would wait a lifetime for her, but it sounded too dramatic and he wasn't sure what she would think, so he didn't.

Andy was true to his word, always there for he was the one person who could be trusted to do what he said, probably part of the reason everyone always liked him, but especially why Becky liked him.

Although it remained fairly uncomplicated with few problems arising, picking Becky up from work was oftentimes a unique experience in patience and hilarity. When he would pick her up, showing up in his Camaro, her boss, Ms. Lally, seemed piqued by his presence which she exhibited by purposely prolonging the closure of the store. So there Andy would sit, sometimes as long as an hour past when the store should have closed, and wait patiently for Becky.

Becky wondered whether it was the boss, Andy, or her that aggravated the situation. Although her boss' mistreatment of her made her think it was herself, her boss' actions made her think it was Andy because the few times he didn't pick her up, her boss closed the store early.

If one knew her boss though, then one surely would have known the issue was with the boss for she was a character. She was a large woman, more so in some areas than others, but particularly in the butt which far exceeded any other part of her body and which seemed to move on its own accord from the rest of her body. She didn't try to hide her size through her clothing, but instead proudly proclaimed her size with clothes exploding in brilliant colors that oftentimes should never have been near each other. Her hair was a similar reflection of her clothes for it was dyed a brilliant red which was always brushed haphazardly outwards. Upon her nose were perched horned-rimmed glasses sprinkled with rhinestones on every corner including the sides that flared outwards and upwards. To top it off, her makeup and nails were just as flamboyant as the rest of her.

For Becky, her boss' mistreatment of her was all too familiar and reminded her of the way others had treated her but it didn't seem to matter now when she knew Andy was waiting for her. Her boss' mistreatment of her was so obvious that oftentimes the other employees could be found defending Becky to the boss, especially when her boss accused her of things she had never done. If anything, her boss' treatment of her made her sad because Becky tried hard to please her boss but no matter what she did it never seemed good enough.

CHAPTER 14
UNSPOKEN WORDS

The changes the new school year brought did not affect them the same. While Becky's world grew to include more people, his began to shrink as his desire to be with her grew stronger, replacing many of the things that had interested him before. With her, he started believing that he could be happy despite his shortcomings and troubled life for she somehow always made him feel that he was his best. She always made him feel a great satisfaction in himself for she never complained or seemed to want for anything more when she was with him. But these feelings of sureness lulled Andy into a sense of security that beguiled him into thinking that there would always be time for them to be together.

But Becky had come to know a world that she had only dreamed about before, but which now seemed to be unfolding before her. Although she had not realized at the time, when Andy had told her she was beautiful something inside of her changed accompanied by her realization that perhaps someone would love her someday.

Her awkwardness and insecurity when around others had disappeared, and she found herself included more often in other people's plans including school events. Things now seemed to come easily for her because she had never really been concerned what others thought of her, so she didn't waste time trying to appease certain people to gain their approval. In fact, what surprised her the most was that she learned they did not talk to her because they thought she was smart and too good for them.

Although she went out often now with her friends, her fervent hope was that she would meet him somewhere , and in amongst the crowd he would see her as more than just the girl next door who needed someone to befriend her. But despite how much she went out, he was never there which she surmised was because he had a girlfriend, which was the most logical she surmised.

For the first time that fall, she began going to dances at the high school although she was never asked to dance. Even as the night wore on and the number of available girls had dwindled, boys would still walk past her without hardly a glance and certainly without a second thought. But for her, her newfound friendships and freedom weren't dimmed by their ignorance of her. Besides, what she didn't want them, what she really hoped for was that Andy would be there and ask her, but he never was. Because he did not know that she waited for him, he never told her that he spent his time working instead so that he could begin planning a future for them.

While the tenor of the high school dances remained the same and she was never asked to dance, she quickly accepted a friend's suggestion one cold night in November to go to a college dance. "Can't be much different," she thought, "nothing to lose certainly."

As she stood there at the dance things seemed to mimic a reoccurrence of the high school dances with no one asking her to dance. Nevertheless, she remained unconcerned as she was used to it and because she filled this void with daydreams that Andy would come and ask her to dance; she was confident, even it out of kindness, he would not walk past her.

Deep in her daydreams, she imagined hearing him say, "Would you like to dance?" and from then on it would all change. "He wouldn't let me go after the dance ended," she imagined, "but would hold me tighter." As deep as her thoughts were, she heard the words echoed clearly. She hesitated, for they no longer seemed to be a part of her dream. Surprised at the repetition, she shook herself from her reverie, and when she looked up, she heard once more the words, "Well, do you want to dance?"

With thoughts of Andy in her head, she at first imagined it was Andy, but instead standing before her was a dark-haired, terribly handsome guy. Slightly disappointed for a moment that it wasn't Andy, she quickly recovered and she could feel a thrill resonating through her entire body. Slipping her hadn into his outstretched hand, she followed him onto the dance floor where the two of them remained for the rest of the night together.

As the last dance finished and the lights were turned up so people would know it was time to leave, the dark handsome stranger asked Becky, "Will you go with me to the movies next Friday?" As she could feel the dizziness, or was it giddiness, that filled her head, she murmured only a few words of acquiescence.

CHAPTER 15
PERPLEXED

Although Andy had always been one of the most popular boys in school, for him it had been a way to escape life at home. Since Becky, he didn't feel the need to run away anymore and he felt he could face any problem with her beside him.

He was no longer interested in the things that he used to be or that other guys in high school typically were. Without a doubt, he now knew with certainty what he wanted in life and who he wanted it with. He had already begun making plans by doing better in school and working hard so that he could own his own business one day.

But it seemed that the harder he worked and the more he focused on these plans, the harder it became to find time to be with Becky which seemed to create a distance between them that had never been there before. Whereas his relationships with others girls seemed superficial and one-dimensional in comparison to his relationship with Becky, it oftentimes left him bewildered because he had never felt like this before. Trouble finding time to be with her and not always knowing what to do left Andy feeling that he was failing rather than building their future together.

With the ever increasing length of times in between when he would see her, his uncertainty and fear had grown which only aggravated his obsessiveness in thinking things over more and more, and second guessing himself as to what he should say, should have said, or should have done.

But when they did see each other, all of his worrying and anxiety seemed to melt away and no longer seemed important. Conjointly, the thoughts and words he had practiced for so long to say to her disappeared from his mind.

But most importantly, it never seemed like the right time or the right place, but afterwards he was left more bewildered and frustrated than ever for having not said what he had wanted to do for so long.

Whereas before Andy always seemed to have somewhere to be, he could now be found sitting home when he wasn't working or school, but Becky now was gone often. On one particular rare Friday night when he didn't have to work, Andy was sitting outside on his porch thinking of her.

He had begun thinking more often that maybe the problem was that their relationship needed more definition, and that he should ask her out on a date though it seemed awkward and strange for their relationship seemed to have surpassed that stage. He mused, "I feel like I have known her forever and so it seems odd to think of asking her for a first date. I don't feel the need to do what others do because what we have is greater than any others. Our love doesn't need to be sustained through pretenses but has a breath of its own."

Deep in his thoughts, he didn't notice Becky as she left her house. When he heard her calling out his name, he looked up and his every other thought halted as he completely captivated by her incessant beauty which seemed every day to be greater than the day before.

Startled, he spurted out without thinking, "I always thought you were the most beautiful girl ever, Becky, but somehow you grow more beautiful every day." With eyes cast down, she shyly replied, "you said that once before."

"Only once? Then I should have said it more, I guess," he said with a smile he couldn't contain.

She walked toward his fence and smiled which always made him feel like he was the most special guy ever. He walked over closer to her, but just then an engine roared up as dark blue Ford truck pulled up. As he turned to look, she slipped away with a wave as she ran off towards the guy getting out of the truck.

Andy's heart sank into his stomach. He had never imagined this happening for he had remained oblivious to the possibility that their love, though unacknowledged. He had thought their love could not change no more than they could change who they were, because who they were was who they were together.

He felt his world and all of his plans crumbling down on him and seemingly vanish in that moment. Watching her leave, he vowed that he could never let another moment escape without her knowing that their futures had   to be one.

CHAPTER 16
A NEW LIFE

As Becky's life had become fuller with friends and activities, she had unintentionally let Andy recede into the background that she had once blended so well into that she had been unnoticed.

But when they did find time together, it was as though nothing had changed. They remained the best of friends which always seemed to lull them both into forgetting their resolve to change things and acting as though nothing had ever changed between them, because it hadn't really.

While Becky continued to go out on more dates that year with some lasting for a short while, she found that the more she dated, the more perplexed and lonelier she seemed to become. "It never felt this way with Andy," she thought. "Being together always seemed so easy and there was always much to share, especially what meant the most to us, our hopes and dreams. But other guys never seem interested in talking about those things and it all seems so difficult."

Because she had always valued his thoughts and opinions, she would ask Andy about other guys for she had become absorbed in her own world and was oblivious to his world, in particular to his feelings for her. Because she seemed to remain ineffectual around other guys and relationships with other guys never seemed to progress, she would turn to the one person she trusted the most and ask him. Sometimes Andy would become highly animated in these discussions but not in a way that answered her questions and certainly not in the way she understood. His responses seemed more to encourage distraction away from other guys. Other times, he would become eerily reticent as though immersed in a gloom in which he offered little insight. He, on the other hand, never talked about any other girl which made Becky wonder, but she feared asking him because she knew he always had many other girlfriends, so she didn't want to ask a question that she already knew the answer to and an answer she didn't want to know.

Despite feeling the same when they were together, the changes in their lives belied their reality. As the year drew to an end, there was growing tension and awkwardness between them which grieved Andy greatly, mostly because of his remorse and chastisement of himself for having second thoughts and not saying what he should have which was aggravated by his increasing confusion and irresoluteness. Still he persisted in his determination to find the words to tell her she was his only one, but it seemed like the time or place was never right.

So in both of their worlds, their bewilderment and frustration continued to mount, but in ways different from each other, but also different from the way their lives had been before when he was popular and she was not. For Andy, he got along easily with other girls, but now he struggled to understand her and his feelings for her. For Becky it was the opposite, for she still understood nothing about guys anymore than she did when she knew none of them. Neither had come any closer to realizing the happiness that seemed such a certain possibility during their summer together, and it seemed that now it was floating away on a current of life that neither of them could control that was pulling them further away from each other.

As the end of their senior year drew near, their lives continued to change as they had all year. For Andy, his plans were to remain in town and work so that eventually he could own his own business and give Becky the best that life could offer. For Becky, it was to go away to college in another town, and so she left and he stayed.

CHAPTER 17
IN OTHER WORLDS

College brought even greater opportunities and challenges
for Becky away from the awkwardness of high school and
the judgmental perceptions of others who hadn't known her.
The number of guys interested in her had continued to grow,
but still, she remained frustrated because it didn't seem that
she was what they wanted, not the way Andy had made her
feel. What she failed to understand was that their idea of a
relationship had no depth as hers with Andy had been, so her
confusion and disillusionment continued to grow.

While she went to college, Andy remained in their hometown
working at a service station. This job actually fit his
personality well as he excelled in repairing cars and he had
always been popular, in large part because he was honest and
always willing to help others. It was not long after that he
acquired his own service station which he later built into the
largest service in town.

As their rapidly changing lives swept them away, they did not stop to contemplate what these changes foretold. It is very sobering when one realizes that there are moments in our lives that fleet past us without our awareness that these moments were the ones manifested as our most important ones. But Andy and Becky were not at a point in their life yet where they felt it necessary to contemplate the effects of how their past would one day determine their future.

Becky did not return often because she worked while attending college, but she always called Andy whenever she did come in. He always seemed to have time for her. Although her life had continued to be filled with many new changes that took her further away from him in every way, there remained a part of her that could never let him go, perhaps even out of fear that if she lost him, she would lose the only real friend she ever had and that she would, once again, be terribly alone in the way she had been before she had met him.

For Andy, his love and commitment to her remained as strong as ever which included his purchase of a diamond ring for her for he had no doubt that there was no one else for him. But time was terribly short when they did get together and there was so much more to do, so it never seemed that the time or place was right.

CHAPTER 18
A HOUSE CLEANING

During spring break, Becky had stopped by Andy's service station but was told he was not there because of a family emergency. She called him and he immediately asked, "Can you come home?"

Although he seemed troubled but not terribly alarmed, she lost no time getting there.   As they sat on the porch as they had done that almost now-forgotten summer, he told her, "Greg, the pharmacist I worked for while in high school is in the hospital. He had been treating himself for stomach pain for over the past six months using medications he got from his pharmacy but apparently the problem was much worse."

Turning to Becky, he asked her, "Will you help me? While there doesn't seem to be a lot I can do for him right now, his house desperately needs a good cleaning." He asked, knowing she would never say no because she never turned away from helping someone else.

They drove to the house, a house of few livable rooms on a road that led nowhere but to a field of rubbled weeds. Greg had lived there his whole life since he had acquired the pharmacy. The age of the house was similarly reflected in his old beat-up, yellow-weathered '73 Vega which had sat much too long alone for Greg rarely drove it as he seldom left the house in his later years.

The same dilapidated state of the car was reflected in the yellowing of the house and decay of its wood and bricks. The front door hung precipitously on its hinges and the windows were outlined by decaying wood that had turned to rot over the many years of being unkempt. Even the glass of the windows had yellowed and weakened from the many, long bitter cold winters leaving great doubt that they did little to preserve heat within the house with the wind easily whistling through them. These windows were covered with sheets that acted as curtains that hung haphazardly, only partially covering the window and letting streaks of light stain the gray, yellowing walls inside which had not seen a paint job in a long time, worn away and scraped in many spots. The second floor of the house had been vacant for a long time and had fallen into a terrible state of disrepair with metal plates staked to them with the hopes that they could preserve the crumbling bricks.

As she walked in, her eyes struggled to adjust for even light from the open door could not overcome the grayness within. It quickly became evident that much of the grayness was due to a heavy, greasy film of soot from too many cigarettes smoked in a too small, enclosed space, and the soot had become so thick and omnipotent that it seemed to permeate even the air itself. When her eyes finally adjusted to the dimness, she felt as though she had walked into a surreal world that stood on the edge of someone's dark and lonely dream.

This house was typical of most small houses built for the miners long ago, too cheaply made to provide any decency, especially long-term, in its living quarters. The meagerness of the house was accentuated by the sparseness of a few sticks of furniture consisting of an old patched couch, a small old TV precariously positioned on a food tray stand, and an old wobbly metal kitchen table with two plastic-covered chairs around it. The bedroom was similarly furnished with a lonely lumpy bed with disheveled grey-colored covers that had never been refreshed with bleach and a nightstand warped too often with circles from the sweat of drinking glasses left too long. Lighting was sparse in all of the rooms and consisted mostly of single bulbs hanging haphazardly from their cords in the middle of the rooms with the exception of one small, terribly smudged table lamp by the bedside. Within the single closet, few clothes hung except for a few plain-colored work clothes. Empty vegetable cans lined the kitchen counters, and the ashtrays were blackened and full of cigarette butts smoked down to the last nudge.

 All of this aroused a great curiosity in Becky as she pondered what kind of life could have survived this and so, after her repeated requests, Andy began to tell Greg's story.

CHAPTER 19
ONE LONELY LIFE

Always typical of Andy to be there for someone when nobody else was, Andy was one of the few, maybe the only one as the years unfolded, who was there for Greg. Andy had worked for him during high school and had kept in touch even after he no longer worked there. Perhaps out of his recognition and hence consideration for the painful isolation that seemed to characterize Greg's life, Andy had always felt a certain obligation to watch over him for he was certain no one else did.

Greg had owned the drugstore for a long time and was its only pharmacist in all of that time. Earlier that morning, Andy had stopped by the drugstore to say hello, but found it closed, something that had never happened before. Andy knew something was wrong and he drove over to Greg's house several blocks away.

Arriving at Greg's house, Andy knocked on the door but heard nothing which confirmed his fear that something was wrong. Creaking the unlocked door open, Andy stared into its darkness, and felt a shudder as the cold within slid down his back.

Still shuddering as he stepped inside, Andy felt around the corner of the door to turn the light switch on, but even the light hanging over the old metal table by its cord seemed to do little to warm the place or make anything clearer.

Feeling his way across the room for the half-shadows did little to show him the way, Andy walked slowly, half fearful that he might stumble but also fearful of what he might find. Seeing and feeling nothing as he crossed, he turned into the bedroom and stumbled to find the one light that stood on the dresser. There lying on the bed he could vaguely see Greg huddled in his blanket and not moving.

When Andy called to him, Greg didn't respond, so Andy moved up close and touched him. With great relief, Andy could feel a faint warmness, but Greg's breathing was inaudible. When he called out Greg's name again and slowly turned him towards him, he could hear moans from Greg who tried to pull his knees up more into his body.

Rushing to the phone, Andy called for an ambulance. Within minutes, the ambulance was there and just as quickly was gone. Andy stayed behind and rummaged through the house, wondering if there was anything there that Greg would need. With the sparseness of things, Andy quickly found a collection of many empty prescription bottles which he gathered for the hospital.   With one last look around the few rooms in this house to be sure he had not missed anything and that nothing else was out of the ordinary, Andy hurried away, for the house left him with a sense of deepening gloom.

By the time Andy had reached the hospital, the doctors still knew little, but Greg's lack of response and ever-increasingly severe stomach pains did not forebode well. Even later, after tests had been run and some treatments attempted, Greg still had little response and the used prescription bottles told little as Greg had been treating himself for a condition that were not allayed by any medication he had given himself over the years.

CHAPTER 20
THE REST OF THE STORY

Now thoroughly engrossed, Becky waited impatiently for
Andy to continue.

"Andy," she said, "what's the rest of the story?"

"What rest of the story do you mean?" he asked.

"The rest of his life," she added. "Nobody lives that way for
no reason. You always liked him well, so why such a scarce
of a life? There had to have been more that he wanted out of
life. You're the only person who knew him anymore for
there doesn't seem to have been anyone else in his life who
cared for him. Surely someone cared about him once for truly
no one can have lived without having loved or been loved at
least once?"

As she said those words, a shiver slid down her back for she
had known that kind of loneliness before, but now she feared
even more that perhaps such loneliness followed a person
throughout their life and ultimately was the final destination
as it had been for Greg.

Andy reflectively and quietly as though the thought of such
utter loneliness also made him shiver, responded, "Yes, he
loved well."

Andy resumed telling Becky the story of Greg. In the 50
years he had owned the drugstore, Greg was almost never
gone. When he had opened his own corner drugstore it was a
time when such stores were the most popular place in town
and came with a soda shop and candy store. So everyone
knew him and everyone liked him. Everyone trusted him and
knew he would always help anyone, even at expense to
himself.

That was until the big drugstores situated themselves near the malls about 15 years later which was closer to the newer parts of town where people moved, and with that Greg was forgotten.   While he had had always been there for them, their lives had taken them away where he no longer existed.

But a few people, including Andy, had remained loyal to Greg but that is the rest of the story and not where this story began.

For Greg, he would have told you that his life started when he met Alicia on the first day of their freshmen year in high school. From the moment he saw her, it seemed as though his life had not begun until then.

Perhaps it was the uncertainty they both felt on starting their first day at high school where everything seemed so big and ominous, and where the first smile they encountered was each other's.

As her smile had given him comfort on that first day, so it did for the rest of the school years. Never a morning passed in which he couldn't wait to see her smile once more, for even on the worst of his days, it always made him feel better.

But there weren't many chances throughout the years for them to talk because their worlds were quite different. While he was more focused on school and took difficult classes, she was the popular girl who was always doing something with friends and involved in lots of school activities. Of course, she was prom queen, but he never went because the only girl he would have asked, which was her, was already going with someone else.

Despite their limited interactions and the great differences between them, his feelings for her never changed nor did his commitment to one day marry her and give her his best always because she deserved nothing less.

In their last year of school, Greg realized the limitations of time and decided he needed to do something, so when the first dance in the fall came around, he went with some friends. He was surprised to see that the boys tended to stand on one side of the room and the girls on the other, something he had never thought would be.   He was even more surprised that Alicia oftentimes stood alone instead of being asked to dance. He had always imagined that every guy would be swarming to dance with her.

As the night wore on and the final dance approached, having danced only a few dances the entire night, Alicia now stood there once again alone. Gripped with fear and having little experience with girls but facing the most important chance of his lifetime, Greg closed his eyes briefly, gulped, and strode across the floor, planting himself in front of her. Hoping that she could not feel his heart beating wildly and his legs shaking, he tried hard to push the words out to ask her to dance, and in some type of form they tumbled out and, although he half-expected her to say no, she answered yes.

While Greg was well liked in high school and admired, he never really dated anyone, but he alone knew the reason because he wanted the best and there was only one girl who was that, Alicia. Holding her in his arms for that final dance fulfilled his greatest dreams and exploded the feelings he had held inside for so long. It was then that he vowed he would never let her go again.

When the dance ended, he regretted deeply having to let go, but he also didn't know what to do next. She seemed as uncertain as he did, so the two of them stood there facing each other. Awkwardly and for his first time ever, he asked a girl out on a date and, once again, she said yes.

CHAPTER 21
STILL TO COME

The year ended with Greg and Alicia having spent most of their free time together, including the few moments they stole in between classes, for she was everything he had dreamed she would be. Being with her though, he was constantly driven by the feeling that one lifetime would never be enough with her and he deeply regretted the time he had already lost in their previous years that he could have spent with her. So, he filled his time thinking of new ways to spend more time with her and things he could for her so that he didn't lose another moment with her.

But as their time together grew, so did familiarity and ennui, leading to their forgetfulness that time never stands still and, more importantly, what is most important in life.

With graduation nearing, they both had their future to plan, and for Greg it meant going to college to become a pharmacist. Although he had always been adept at the sciences and knew this job would be a perfect fit for him, his main concern was that he wanted to be able to give Alicia the best of everything so that she should never want for anything in her life. Alicia was going to remain at home and work, waiting for him.

Having never dated any other girls and being a man of few words, Greg oftentimes did not comprehend the need for nor display the typical responses of someone in love. This left him and Alicia oftentimes with second thoughts, questioning what they should say. Despite their doubts, though, they always seemed certain they would always be there for each other for they had loved no other.

Besides, there was much more else to worry about at this time when they were graduating and making big changes in

their lives. As he left to go to college, he remained assured
that he had no doubts about their future together, and he was
certain she had none either.

While the distance from the college to their home town
strengthened Greg's love and commitment for her, for Alicia
it began to foster doubts. These doubts were compounded by
her increasing loneliness with the realization that their two
worlds were becoming quite different, and that when he
returned she might not be good enough for him. Her doubts
were further aggravated by the diminishing number of letters
he wrote as his studies intensified and time became harder to
find to write.

With her increasing loneliness and doubts, Alicia began
looking elsewhere for something to fill her time with, so she

began going out with friends and just as quickly other guys began paying her the attention she missed.

Finally, Greg's last year at college had ended and he headed home to begin working as a pharmacist at a local drugstore, thus fulfilling all of his plans. As he stepped off the plane in his hometown, he felt in his pocket for the small box in which the diamond ring he had bought for her waited.

CHAPTER 22
NEVER MEANING TO BE SAID

As he stepped off the plane and saw her, his first thoughts were of how Alicia was even more beautiful than ever. He felt his love for her rush over him, leaving him to wonder how he had ever lasted those years in college away from her and why he had not asked her to marry him for every first moment he had seen her.

As he got closer to her, she seemed preoccupied, almost distant, and a sickening doubt began to overwhelm him although he tried hard to push it away. He pulled her close to him, but she slipped away quickly. Instead she began talking exuberantly about many things, most of which he was not really interested at this time, but he laughed nonetheless whether it was at her exuberance or to allay his growing uneasiness.

He thought they were going to spend all of their time together for now on, and he had spent much time trying to think of the most romantic way to ask her to marry him for nothing but the best would be good enough for her. But she began apologizing profusely and, as she drove up to his house, told him she had made other plans because she knew that he had much else to do since he had just gotten back. Without giving him any time to protest, she hurried off.

And so all of her time in the next few days seemed to go, and Greg found it impossible to find the time he wanted to spend with her which greatly undermined his chance to ask her to marry him. But his frustration and regret grew with every day passing and he began to worry that maybe he would never have the chance to say what he had wanted to say every time he was with her but which he never had.

Whereas everything with Alicia had always seemed so easy, it now had become more difficult than anything he had ever known, but he remained determined to tell her once more that he loved her and ask her to marry him.

Still having not been able to talk to her and having stayed up all night with the sense of urgency and desperation gnawing at him, he stood outside her house early in the morning. When she came out, fearful of hesitating any longer, he stood in front of her and said, "Alicia, you know I love you more than anyone else." But he didn't finish what he wanted to say most of all for she looked more embarrassed than pleased, and looking down at the ground, she said, "I am marrying someone else."

CHAPTER 23
A LIFE NOT LIVED

And so, Greg never bothered her again. His life quickly became a routine in which he went to work and back home alone again.   With nothing else but his hard work, he quickly became the owner of the drugstore.

There was one exception to his routine though, and that was when he would drive by where she worked, or if later at night where she lived, and eventually where she picked her children up from school so that he could see her one more time, even if from a distance. Otherwise, he avoided meeting her because she seemed happy, and he didn't want to disturb her happiness because that is what he had always wanted the most for her, but what it did do was isolate him further from everyone else.

Now here he lay in the hospital losing his last chance to ever see her again for he knew now that his self-medicating had failed to allay his cancer.

EPILOGUE

While sometimes we may wish that some moments would stand still, they never do but, in truth, time passes much too quickly, oftentimes leaving no more chances to make the choices never made and perchance to regain what was once lost.

Greg never returned home and died of cancer shortly thereafter, and Becky's and Andy's lives went in different directions as they had been seeming to do.

Many years later, having two grown daughters, Becky lived far away on her own. Although she had tried hard, her marriage didn't work for it seemed that she never had been the kind of woman that men fell in love with, so she never remarried. On her better days, she wondered if perhaps her other relationships had never worked with other guys because, she thought, "Perhaps I didn't have my heart to give away because once, a long time ago in the beginning, I had already given it to another."

It was a warm December day where she lived now when she received an unexpected phone call from her sister telling her that Andy had died unexpectedly the day before from a heart attack. Though Becky had never seen Andy again after she had moved away, she had known that he had married late in life but after a short time had divorced and never married again and never had any children, but she knew little else.

But that didn't mean that she had not thought of him often. In fact she still had the letter she had written many years before but never sent because she believed he would have thought she was foolish – foolish because she had always hoped that he would be the one to whom she mattered the most. Without him knowing and her never telling him, he had always been the one who had breathed the hope of life into her once-lonely existence, a loneliness she had never known again as long as she knew he was alive. But now he was gone and she felt that horrible feeling of loneliness once again rush over her, sinking deep into her being with a sense of a growing empty hole that once had been filled, but was never to be filled again for no one could ever fill that hole as he had.

A week after the phone call, Becky was greatly surprised by a package in the mail. Completely mystified, she stood before it for what seemed like an eternity, or perhaps she wanted it to seem like eternity, for the return address was from Andy.

Finally, with shaking hands and her heart beating wildly, she opened it. Within the box was another box and a note on top. She slowly opened the note, trying to peek and anticipate what words might appear.   The words written there were few and simple, "You were always the most beautiful woman I ever knew and I never loved any other but you. Please marry me."

She could do nothing more as her body shook with her sobs for all of the pain and loneliness of her life seemed to swell up in that moment of realization that everything she had ever hoped for had always been there for the taking, but she was equally overwhelmed by her sorrow for never having known this.

As her tears cleared and she could make out the shape of the small box, she struggled to open it as her finger shook, and through the cloudiness in her eyes she saw his diamond ring. For all that had not been said or done between them, Andy had been able to snatch his greatest desire from the grips of death and with her "yes" eternalized their love forever.

The End.